Katie Morag
and the Riddles

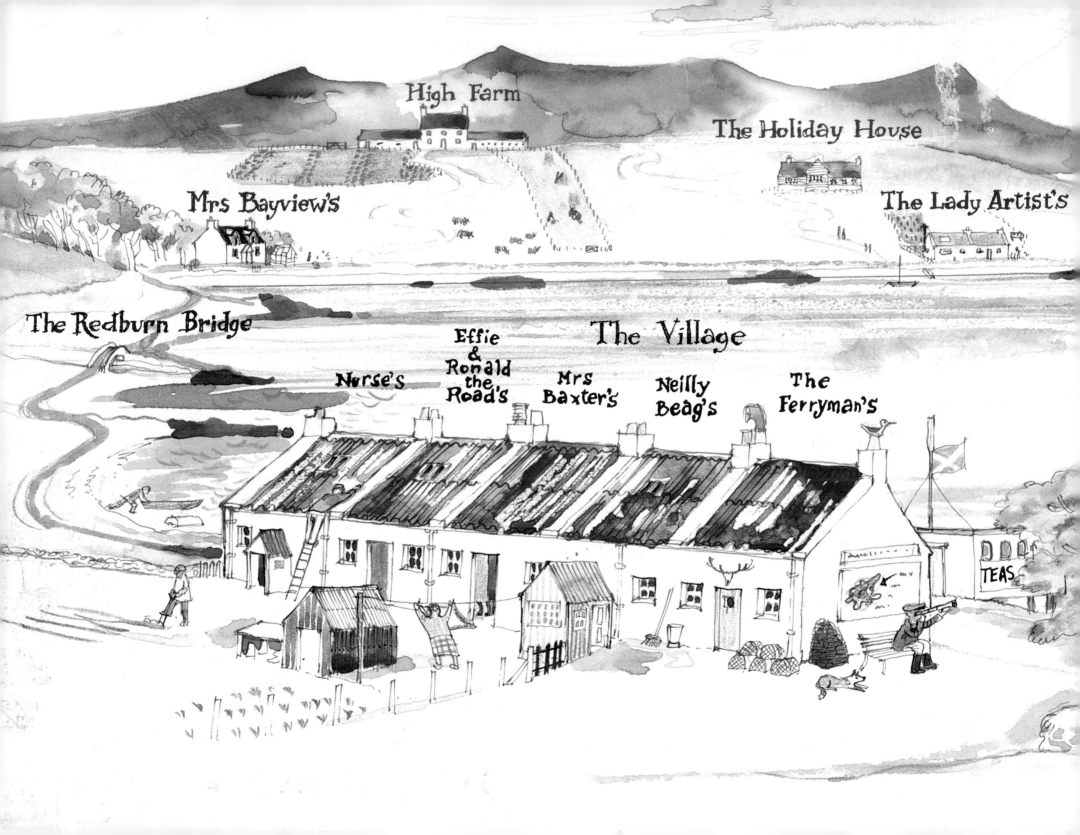

Grannie's

The Mainland

The New Pier

OBAN TIMES GET YOUR COPY HERE

ISLE of STRUAY SHOP & POST OFFICE

BISTRO

The Jetty

TO THE NEW PIER

CRAFTS

WELCOME

WEST HIGHLAND FREE PRESS

ORDER NOW

LITTE

The Shop & Post Office

For Sophie who knows all about school and Kirsty who soon will

KATIE MORAG AND THE RIDDLES
A RED FOX BOOK 978 1 849 41092 2

First published in Great Britain by The Bodley Head, an imprint of
Random House Children's Publishers UK A Random House Group Company

Bodley Head edition published 2001
Red Fox edition published 2002
This Red Fox edition published 2010

5 7 9 10 8 6 4

Copyright © Mairi Hedderwick 2001

The right of Mairi Hedderwick to be identified as the author and illustrator of this work has been
asserted in accordance with the Copyright, Designs and Patents Act 1988.

Red Fox Books are published by Random House Children's Publishers UK,
61-63 Uxbridge Road, London W5 5SA

www.**randomhousechildrens**.co.uk
www.**randomhouse**.co.uk

Addresses for companies within The Random House Group Limited can be found at:
www.**randomhouse**.co.uk/offices.htm

THE RANDOM HOUSE GROUP Limited Reg. No. 954009

A CIP catalogue record for this book is available from the British Library

Printed in Italy

The Random House Group Limited supports The Forest Stewardship Council® (FSC®), the leading
international forest-certification organisation. Our books carrying the FSC label are printed on FSC®-certified paper.
FSC is the only forest-certification scheme supported by the leading environmental organisations, including Greenpeace.
Our paper procurement policy can be found at www.randomhouse.co.uk/environment.

Katie Morag
and the Riddles

Mairi Hedderwick

RED FOX

"I hate school!" thought Katie Morag.

The Big Boy Cousins were making an oil rig and Agnes was allowed to help. The teacher had asked Katie Morag for the second day running to show the wee ones how to thread beads.

"Baby stuff!" she muttered. "Everyone else gets better things to do than me!" Katie Morag was very peeved.

But Liam was delighted that his big sister had come to help.

"I have got a sore tummy," said Katie Morag next morning when the family was at breakfast.

"Eat up your porridge and it will go away," said her mother, Mrs McColl. "Hurry up or you'll be late for school. You haven't even got your clothes on yet! HURRY UP!"

"Is it really sore?" asked her father, Mr McColl.

"REALLY sore," wailed Katie Morag.

Mr McColl tucked Katie Morag up in her parents' bed. It was lovely snuggling down under the big duvet and hearing Liam going off to school with Mrs McColl and the baby in the pushchair. She listened to Mr McColl humming to himself as he tidied the kitchen before going downstairs to open up the Shop and Post Office.

It was so peaceful and quiet being left alone.

Katie Morag soon got bored, however. She got out of bed, her sore tummy quite gone, and put on her mother's best shoes and lipstick and perfume. Mrs McColl's nightie was like a ball gown; her necklace so pretty.

But as Katie Morag pirouetted round the room the thread of Mrs McColl's favourite necklace broke.

In a panic, Katie Morag collected the scattered beads.
She ran to her room and hid them in her secret hiding place.
She would get the special needle and bead thread from school.
She was desperate to go to school now.

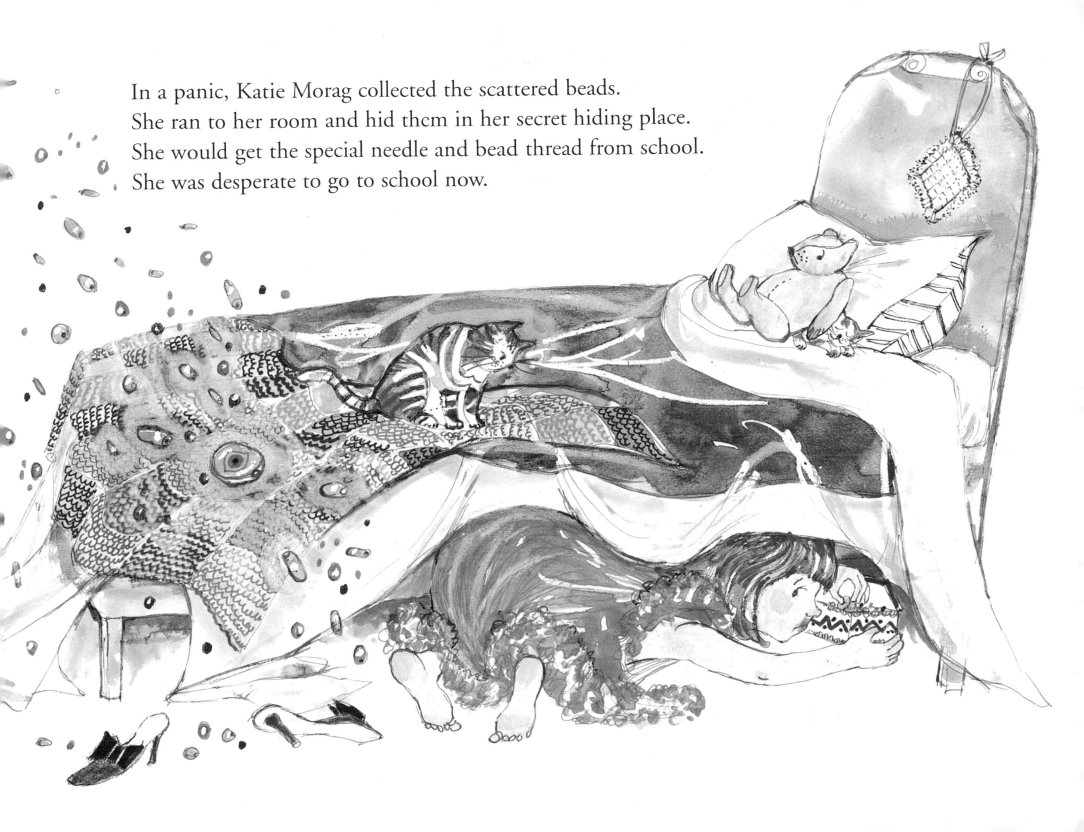

Next day the Teacher said that Jamie could help the wee ones. "PLEASE let me,"
Katie Morag pleaded. "I LOVE helping the wee ones!"
   "Really?" asked the Teacher, in amazement.
   "Give me the needle and thread!" Katie Morag whispered to her little brother.
   But Liam said, in a loud voice, "Go away, Katie Morag! I can do it myself!"

"You give them to ME!" screeched Katie Morag.

"Katie Morag!" frowned the Teacher. "Go back to your seat!"

Things got worse for Katie Morag. Because she was so miserable deep down inside she was horrible now to the Big Boy Cousins and Agnes. So they were horrible to her.

After lunch there was a terrible squabble in the playground.

"Katie Morag started it!" accused the Big Boy Cousins.

"You big ones should know how to behave better!" said the Teacher, exasperated. "For your homework I want you all to work together to find the answers to these riddles by Monday."

"I don't understand any of this," growled Hector, the biggest Big Boy Cousin, when he tried to make sense of the riddles. "Listen. It's glaikit blethers:

No. 1: *The land was white,*
The seed was black;
It will take a good scholar
To riddle me that.

No. 2: *As round as an apple,*
As deep as a pail;
It never cries out,
Till it's caught by its tail.

No. 3: *Four stiff-standers,*
Four dilly-danders,
Two lookers,
Two crookers,
And a wig wag.

No 4: *A wee, wee man*
In a dark red coat;
A staff in my hand,
And a stone in my throat.
Who am I?"

"This is all your fault, Katie Morag!" The Cousins and Agnes glowered at her.

"I'll get the answers," mumbled Katie Morag, miserably, hoping they would leave her alone. And they did, running off with whoops of joy. "See you Monday morning then, with all the answers, Katie Morag!"

Katie Morag was grateful when Liam took her hand on the slow journey home.

WELCOME TO TRUAY SCHOOL

The next day, Katie Morag went to see Grannie Island.

"So, Miss Mopus, what is the long face for?" Grannie Island asked.
Katie Morag told Grannie Island her troubles.
But she said nothing about the necklace.

"Well, you have come to the right place for the first riddle," said Grannie Island.

> *The land was white,*
> *The seed was black;*
> *It will take a good scholar*
> *To riddle me that.*

"Look at the book on my knee!" nudged Grannie Island.
Katie Morag looked hard; the white pages were like square fields and the letters like black seeds planted in rows!
"Books don't always have answers," mused Grannie Island. "Sometimes people know answers better…"

As round as an apple, As deep as a pail; It never cries out, Till it's caught by its tail.

No. 2

Four stiff-standers, Four dilly-danders, Two lookers, Two crookers, And a wig wag.

No. 3

Katie Morag told everyone she met on the way home all about the riddles.

The Lady Artist was polishing her big doorbell. "Stop pulling its tail, silly old goat! What a clanging, Katie Morag!"

Mr McMaster was herding Dilly, the cow, into the byre for milking. "Grab the pail, Katie Morag, and you can help!"

A wee wee man, In a dark red coat; A staff in my hand, and a stone in my throat. Who am I?

No. 4

Mrs Bayview was in her orchard picking dark red cherries. "Careful you don't swallow a stone, Katie Morag!"

RIDDLE No. 4

Katie Morag had found the answers to all the riddles! Have you?

Katie Morag was first at school on Monday morning. The Big Boy Cousins and Agnes were worried that she did not have all the answers to the riddles.

Katie Morag handed over the answers with a big grin.

"Well done!" smiled the Teacher. "I am glad you worked together so well. I hope that is the end of all the squabbling?"

"Oh, yes!" replied The Big Boy Cousins and Agnes, relieved. "We think Katie Morag is great. She worked the hardest of all!"

At the end of the day, Katie Morag asked if she could borrow the special needle and thread for making necklaces. "Of course!" smiled the Teacher. Once Katie Morag got Mrs McColl's necklace mended, all her troubles would be over.

Katie Morag made Liam run all the way home. She raced up to her bedroom but Mrs McColl's beads were not in the hiding place. They were gone!

Oh dear, what if her mother had found them? Would she think Katie Morag had stolen them? Oh dear, oh dearic me! Everything was awful again. Mrs McColl often wore that necklace in the evenings…

But someone had already mended Mrs McColl's necklace!

Mrs McColl asked Liam how he had got on at school. "I threaded the beads without any help from Katie Morag," Liam said proudly.

"I'm glad that sore tummy of yours has gone away, Katie Morag," winked Mr McColl.

"So am I," laughed Katie Morag. "I'm looking forward to school tomorrow." She was feeling ever so much better.

"Aye, she has the making of a good scholar, has our Katie Morag," smiled Grannie Island.

And there were the Big Boy Cousins and Agnes at the door waiting to play.

Join Katie Morag on more adventures!